THE USBORNE
BOOK OF
EVERYDAY
WORDS
in French

Designer and modelmaker: Jo Litchfield

Editors: Rebecca Treays, Kate Needham and Lisa Miles
French language consultant: Lorraine Beurton-Sharp
Photography: Howard Allman
Modelmaker: Stefan Barnett
Managing Editor: Felicity Brooks
Managing Designer: Mary Cartwright
Photographic manipulation and design: Michael Wheatley

With thanks to Inscribe Ltd. and Eberhard Faber for providing the Fimo® modeling material

Everyday Words is a stimulating and lively wordfinder for young children. Each page shows familiar scenes from the world around us, providing plenty of opportunity for talking and sharing. Small, labeled pictures throughout the book tell you the words for things in French.

There are a number of hidden objects to find in every big scene. A small picture shows what to look for, and children can look up the French word for the numbers on page 43.

Above all, this bright and busy book will give children hours of enjoyment and a love of reading that will last.

La famille

la soeur   le frère   la fille   le père   le fils   la mère

le chat   la grand-mère   le grand-père   le chien

le petit-fils   la petite-fille

La ville

 Trouve quinze voitures

la station-service

le supermarché

les magasins

l'hôpital

la piscine

l'école

le parking

le cinéma

le pont

5

La rue

 Trouve douze oiseaux

la boulangerie

le serveur

l'agent de police

la pharmacie

la poussette

l'arrêt de bus

6

 la boucherie

 le chien

 le café

 la planche à roulettes

 le pompier

 le landau

 le lampadaire

 la poste

 le chat

 le boulanger

La maison

Trouve huit tasses

la porte

la poignée

la moquette

le toit

la rampe

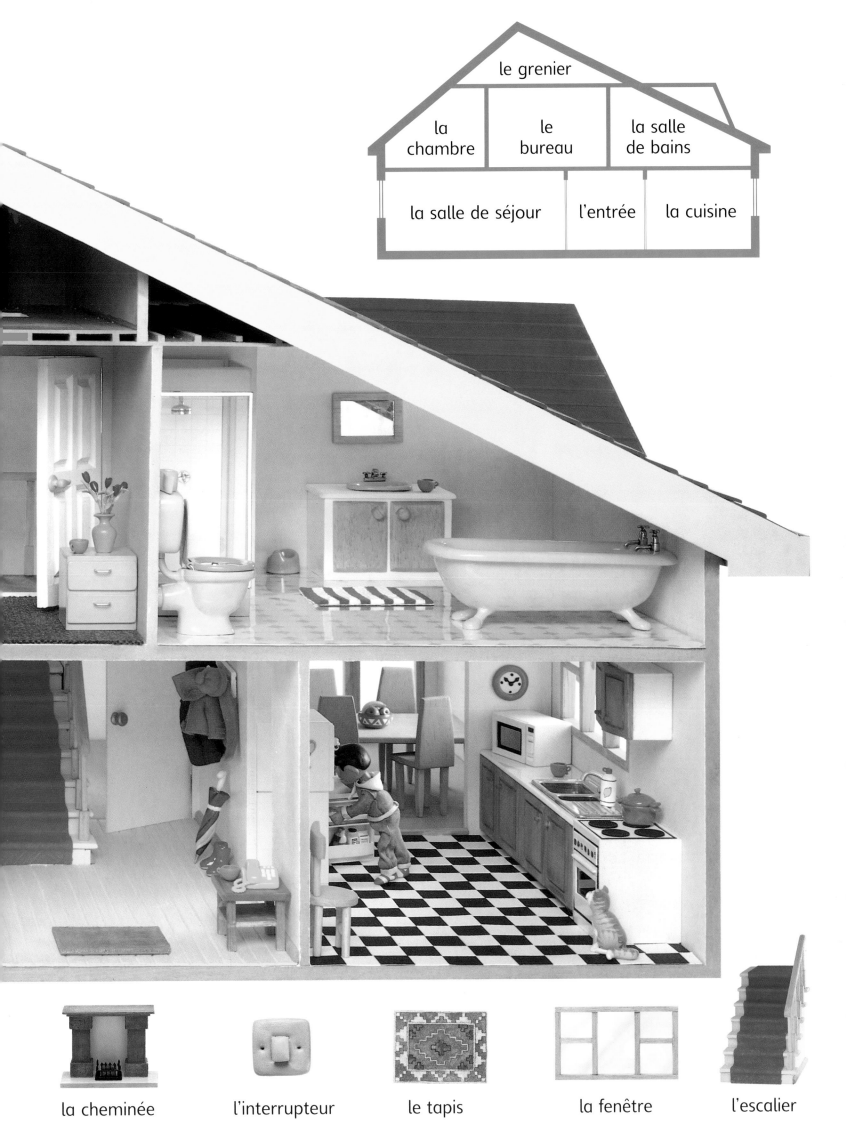

le grenier

la chambre

le bureau

la salle de bains

la salle de séjour

l'entrée

la cuisine

la cheminée

l'interrupteur

le tapis

la fenêtre

l'escalier

q

Le jardin

Trouve dix-sept vers de terre

la chenille

le pot de fleurs

l'abeille

la binette

l'os

la limace

la coccinelle

la feuille

l'escargot

la fourmi

le râteau

la niche

l'arbre

le barbecue

le papillon

la brouette

les graines

le nid

la tondeuse

11

La cuisine

 Trouve dix tomates

l'évier

le couteau

le lave-linge

le grille-pain

la chaise

la soucoupe

la table

la tasse

la poêle

le four à micro-ondes

la fourchette

la passoire

la cuisinière

la cuillère

la pelle
à ordures

le lave-
vaisselle

l'assiette

la casserole

la carafe

le bol

le réfrigérateur

La nourriture

le biscuit · le pain

les pâtes · le riz · la farine · les céréales

le jus de fruits · le sachet de thé · le café · le sucre

le lait · la crème · le beurre · l'œuf · le fromage · le yaourt

le poulet · la crevette · la saucisse · la poitrine fumée · le poisson · le saucisson

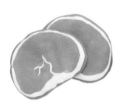   

le jambon · la soupe · la pizza · le sel · le poivre · la moutarde

le ketchup · le miel · la confiture · les raisins secs · les cacahuètes · l'eau

l'ananas   la poire   le citron vert   le citron   la pêche   l'abricot

la cerise   la banane   la fraise   la framboise   la mangue   le pamplemousse

la prune   la noix de coco   l'orange   la pastèque   le melon   le raisin

la pomme   le kiwi   la tomate   l'avocat   la pomme de terre   les haricots verts

la courgette   le chou   l'oignon   le champignon   la carotte   l'aubergine

le poireau   le brocoli   le chou-fleur   les petits pois   les épinards   la betterave

la laitue   le céleri   le maïs   le concombre   le piment rouge   le poivron

15

La salle de séjour

 Trouve six cassettes

 le CD

le porte-monnaie

le fauteuil

l'aspirateur

la cassette vidéo

 le canapé

 le magnétoscope

la mini-chaîne

le puzzle

la télévision

la flûte

la fleur

le compotier

le tambourin

le plateau

le coussin

le piano

le casque stéréo

Le bureau

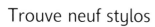 Trouve neuf stylos

 le bureau

 l'ordinateur

 le téléphone

 le magazine

 la guitare

 la plante verte

 le livre

 le crayon cire

 la photo

La salle de bains

 Trouve trois bateaux

le savon

le lavabo

la serviette

la bonde

les toilettes

la baignoire

le papier WC

le peigne

le shampooing

la douche

La chambre

 Trouve quatre araignées

le crocodile

la trompette

la commode

le robot

le lit

l'ours en peluche

la fusée

la poupée

le tambour

le vaisseau spatial

l'éléphant

la cassette

le serpent

le réveil

la marionnette

la table de nuit

le lion

la couverture

la girafe

les cartes

21

Dans la maison

le dentifrice

la brosse à dents

le journal

la lettre

le store

le rideau

la couette

l'oreiller

l'album photos

la planche à
repasser

le fer à repasser

la machine
à coudre

le vase

la souris

le pot

l'éponge

le robinet

la brosse à cheveux

le miroir

la poubelle

le liquide vaisselle

la calculatrice

les jouets

la lampe

Les transports

l'ambulance

le camion de pompiers

la voiture de police

l'hélicoptère

le camion

la voiture

la pelleteuse

la trottinette

le bateau

le canoë

la caravane

l'avion

la montgolfière

le tracteur

le taxi

le vélo

l'autobus

la moto

le sous-marin

le train

la voiture de course

la camionnette

le téléphérique

la voiture de sport

La ferme

 Trouve cinq chatons

le cochonnet   le cochon

l'oie

le taureau

la vache

le veau

le coq   le poussin   la poule

24

la grange

le lapin

le mouton

l'agneau

la mare

l'âne

la chèvre

le fermier

le dindon

la barrière

le caneton

le canard

le chiot

le cheval

La salle de classe

 Trouve vingt crayons cire

 le taille-crayon

 le chevalet

 le stylo à encre

 le papier

 le feutre

 la craie

 le portemanteau

les ciseaux

l'ardoise

26

la ficelle

le tabouret

le crayon

la gomme

le ruban adhésif

la colle

les cubes

la peinture

le pinceau

l'instituteur

la pendule

le cahier

la règle

La fête

 Trouve onze pommes

 le magnétophone

 le cadeau

le pirate

le cow-boy

le docteur

 les chips

 le pop-corn

le ballon

le ruban

le gâteau

le chocolat

la glace

la carte

la ballerine

la sirène

l'astronaute

le bonbon

la bougie

la paille

la chaise haute

le clown

29

Le camping

 Trouve deux ours en peluche

la valise

la tente

l'appareil photo

la radio

le sac à dos

la carte d'identité

la torche

la pellicule photo

l'argent

le ballon de football

le parapluie

la carte

les jumelles

le chaton

le billet

Les vêtements

le tee-shirt

le jean

la salopette

la robe

la jupe

le collant

le pyjama

le peignoir

le maillot
de corps

le bavoir

le pull-over

le sweat-shirt

le gilet

le pantalon

le tablier

la chemise

le manteau

le survêtement

32

 le caleçon

 le slip

 le maillot de bain

 le slip de bain

 le maillot deux-pièces

 la cravate

 la ceinture

 les bretelles

 la fermeture éclair

 le bouton

 l'écharpe

 les lunettes

 les lunettes de soleil

 le badge

 la montre

 la chaussette

 le gant

 le chapeau

 la casquette

 le casque

 la bottine

 la chaussure de sport

 le chausson de danse

 la pantoufle

 la chaussure

la sandale

L'atelier

 Trouve treize souris

la boîte à outils

l'arrosoir

le clou

le marteau

le canif

le tournevis

le pot

l'araignée

34

la scie

l'étau

la clé

le ver de terre

le seau

la bêche

l'allumette

le carton

la roue

le tuyau d'arrosage

la corde

le papillon de nuit

la clé plate

le balai

35

Le jardin public

 Trouve sept ballons de football

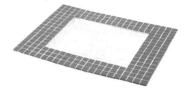

la pataugeoire

le garçon

l'oiseau

 le sandwich

 la raquette de tennis

 le hamburger

 le cerf-volant

 le bébé

 le hot dog

 les frites

 le fauteuil roulant

 la fille

 les balançoires

 la bascule

 le tourniquet

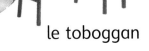 le toboggan

Le corps

la tête

l'oreille

la langue

le nez

la bouche

les dents

l'oeil

le dos

le ventre

le nombril

le bras

la jambe

le coude

le genou

la main

le pied

le doigt

le pouce

le derrière

les cheveux longs

les cheveux courts

les cheveux frisés

les cheveux raides

Les actions

dormir

faire du vélo

monter à cheval

sourire

rire

pleurer

chanter

marcher

courir

sauter

jouer au ballon

40

écrire   peindre   dessiner   lire   découper   coller

être assis   être debout   pousser   tirer

manger   boire   se laver   s'embrasser   faire signe

Les formes

 l'ovale

 le cercle

 le croissant

 le triangle

 le rectangle

 le carré

 l'étoile

Les couleurs

 rouge

 jaune

 gris

 violet

 blanc

 vert

 noir

 rose

 marron

 bleu

orange

42

Les nombres

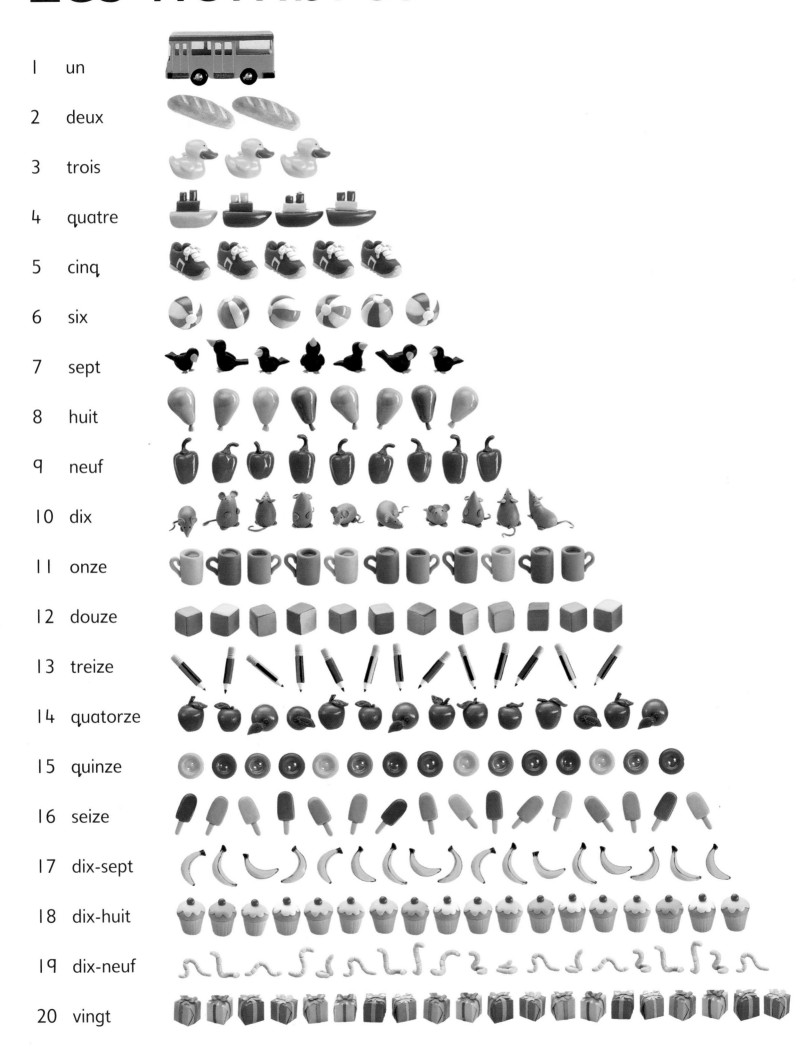

1 un

2 deux

3 trois

4 quatre

5 cinq

6 six

7 sept

8 huit

9 neuf

10 dix

11 onze

12 douze

13 treize

14 quatorze

15 quinze

16 seize

17 dix-sept

18 dix-huit

19 dix-neuf

20 vingt

Word list

In this list, you can find all the French words in this book. They are listed in alphabetical order. Next to each one, you can see its pronunciation guide (how to say it) in letters *like this*, and then its English translation.

French nouns (words for objects) are either masculine or feminine. In the list, each one has **le**, **la**, **l'** or **les** in front of it. These all mean "the". The words with **le** are masculine, those with **la** are feminine.

French nouns that begin with "a", "e", "i", "o" or "u", and many that begin with an "h", have **l'** in front of them. At the end, you will see **(m)** or **(f)** to show if the word is masculine or feminine. Words with **les** in front of them are plural, which means more than one of something, for example "cats". These are also followed by **(m)** or **(f)**.

About French pronunciation

Read each pronunciation as if it were an English word, but remember the following points about how French words are said:

● The French **j** is said like the "s" in "treasure".

● When you see (n) or (m) in a pronunciation, you should barely say the "n" or the "m". Say the letter that comes before it through your nose, as if you have a cold.

● The French **r** is made at the back of the throat. It sounds a little like gargling.

● The French **u** is not like any sound in English. It is a little like a cross between the "ew" of "few" and the "oo" of "food". To say it, round your lips to say "oo" and then try to say "ee". The pronunciations use the letters "ew" to show this sound.

a

l'abeille (f)	*labbaye*	bee
l'abricot (m)	*labreeko*	apricot
les actions (f)	*layz-ak-see-o(n)*	actions
l'agent de police (m)	*la-jo(n) duh poleess*	policeman
l'agneau (m)	*lan-yo*	lamb
l'album photos (m)	*lalbom foto*	photo album
l'allumette (f)	*la-lewmett*	match
l'ambulance (f)	*lo(m)bewlan(n)ss*	ambulance
l'ananas (m)	*la-na-na*	pineapple
l'âne (m)	*lan*	donkey
l'appareil photo (m)	*lappa-ray foto*	camera
l'araignée (f)	*la-renn-yay*	spider
les araignées (f)	*layz a-renn-yay*	spiders
l'arbre (m)	*lar-br*	tree
l'ardoise (f)	*lardwaz*	chalkboard
l'argent (m)	*lar-jo(n)*	money
l'arrêt de bus (m)	*laray duh bewss*	bus stop
l'arrosoir (m)	*la-rozwar*	watering can
l'aspirateur (m)	*lass-peera-ter*	vacuum cleaner
l'assiette (f)	*lassee-yet*	plate
l'astronaute (m/f)	*lass-tronnawt*	spaceman/woman
l'atelier (m)	*lattuh-lee-yay*	workshop
l'aubergine (f)	*lo-bair-jeen*	eggplant
l'autobus (m)	*lotto-bewss*	bus
l'avion (m)	*lav-yo(n)*	airplane
l'avocat (m)	*lavoka*	avocado

b

le badge	*luh badj*	pin
la baignoire	*la bay-nwar*	bathtub
le balai	*luh ballay*	broom
les balançoires (f)	*lay ballo(n)-swar*	swings
la ballerine	*la ball-uh-reen*	ballerina
le ballon	*luh ballo(n)*	balloon/ball
le ballon de football	*luh ballo(n) duh foot-bol*	soccer ball
les ballons de football	*lay ballo(n) duh foot-bol*	soccer balls
la banane	*la ban-an*	banana
le barbecue	*luh bar-buh-kew*	barbecue grill
la barrière	*la bar-yair*	gate
la bascule	*la baskewl*	seesaw
le bateau	*luh batto*	boat
les bateaux (m)	*lay batto*	boats
le bavoir	*luh bavwar*	bib
le bébé	*luh bebay*	baby
la bêche	*la besh*	shovel
la betterave	*la bet-rav*	beets
le beurre	*luh ber*	butter
le billet	*luh bee-yay*	ticket
la binette	*la beennet*	shovel
le biscuit	*luh beess-kwee*	cookie
blanc	*blo(n)*	white
bleu	*bluh*	blue
boire	*bwar*	to drink
la boîte à outils	*la bwa-ta-ootee*	toolbox
le bol	*luh bol*	bowl
le bonbon	*luh bo(n)bo(n)*	candy
la bonde	*la bond*	plug
la bottine	*la bo-teen*	boot
la bouche	*la boosh*	mouth
la boucherie	*la boosh-ree*	butcher's shop
la bougie	*la boo-jee*	candle
le boulanger	*luh boolo(n)-jay*	baker (man)
la boulangerie	*la boolo(n)j-ree*	baker's shop
le bouton	*luh boo-to(n)*	button
le bras	*luh bra*	arm
les bretelles (f)	*lay bruh-tell*	suspenders
le brocoli	*luh bro-ko-lee*	broccoli
la brosse à cheveux	*la brossa-shuh-vuh*	hairbrush
la brosse à dents	*la brossa-do(n)*	toothbrush
la brouette	*la broo-ett*	wheelbarrow
le bureau	*luh bew-ro*	study/desk

c			
les cacahuètes (f)	lay ka-ka-wet	peanuts
le cadeau	luh kaddo	present (gift)
le café	luh kaffay	café/coffee
le cahier	luh ka-yay	notebook
la calculatrice	la kalkew-latreess	calculator
le caleçon	luh kalson	boxer shorts
le camion	luh kam-yo(n)	truck
le camion de pompiers	luh kam-yo(n) duh po(m)p-yay	fire engine
la camionnette	la kam-yonnett	delivery van
le camping	luh ko(m)peeng	campsite
le canapé	luh kannapay	sofa
le canard	luh kannar	duck
le caneton	luh kan-to(n)	duckling
le canif	luh kanneef	pocketknife
le canoë	luh kanno-ay	kayak
la carafe	la ka-raf	jug
la caravane	la ka-ra-van	trailer
la carotte	la ka-rot	carrot
le carré	luh karray	square
la carte	la kart	map/card
la carte d'identité	la kart deedo(n)-teetai	identity card
les cartes (f)	lay kart	playing cards
le carton	luh kar-to(n)	cardboard box
le casque	luh kask	helmet
le casque stéréo	luh kask stair-ayo	headphones
la casquette	la kass-ket	cap
la casserole	la kass-rol	saucepan
la cassette	la kassett	cassette
la cassette vidéo	la kassett veeday-o	video tape
les cassettes (f)	lay kassett	cassettes
le CD	luh say-day	CD
la ceinture	la sa(n)tewr	belt
le céleri	luh sell-ree	celery
le cercle	luh sairkl	circle
les céréales (f)	lai sair-ayal	cereal
le cerf-volant	luh sair vollo(n)	kite
la cerise	la suh-reez	cherry
la chaise	la shez	chair
la chaise haute	la shez owt	highchair
la chambre	la sho(m)br	bedroom
le champignon	luh sho(m)peen-yo(n)	mushroom
chanter	sho(n)tay	to sing
le chapeau	luh shappo	hat
le chat	luh sha	cat
le chaton	luh shatto(n)	kitten
les chatons	lay shatto(n)	kittens
la chaussette	la shossett	sock
le chausson de danse	luh shosso(n) duh do(n)ss	ballet shoe
la chaussure	la shossewr	shoe
la chaussure de sport	la shossewr duh spor	tennis shoe
la cheminée	la shuh-meenai	chimney
la chemise	la shuh-meez	shirt
la chenille	la shuh-nee-yuh	caterpillar
le cheval	luh shuh-val	horse
les cheveux (m)	lay shuh-vuh	hair
les cheveux courts (m)	lay shuh-vuh koor	short hair
les cheveux frisés (m)	lay shuh-vuh free-zai	curly hair
les cheveux longs (m)	lay shuh-vuh lo(n)	long hair
les cheveux raides (m)	lay shuh-vuh red	straight hair
la chèvre	la shevr	goat
le chien	luh shee-a(n)	dog
le chiot	luh shee-o	puppy
les chips (f)	lay sheeps	French fries
le chocolat	luh sho-ko-la	chocolate
le chou	luh shoo	cabbage
le chou-fleur	luh shoo-fler	cauliflower
le cinéma	luh seenayma	movie theater
cinq	sank	five
les ciseaux (m)	lay see-zo	scissors
le citron	luh seetro(n)	lemon
le citron vert	luh seetro(n) vair	lime
la clé	la klay	key
la clé plate	la klay plat	wrench
le clou	luh kloo	nail
le clown	luh kloon	clown
la coccinelle	la kok-see-nell	ladybug
le cochon	luh kosho(n)	pig
le cochonnet	luh koshon-ay	piglet
le collant	luh ko-lo(n)	tights
la colle	la kol	glue
coller	ko-lay	to stick
la commode	la ko-mod	chest of drawers
le compotier	luh ko(m)pot-yay	fruit bowl
le concombre	luh ko(n)-ko(m)br	cucumber
la confiture	la ko(n)fee-tewr	jelly
le coq	luh kok	rooster
la corde	la kord	rope
le corps	luh kor	body
le coude	luh kood	elbow
la couette	la koo-ett	comforter
les couleurs (f)	lay koo-ler	colors
la courgette	la koorjet	zucchini
courir	kooreer	to run
le coussin	luh koo-sa(n)	cushion
le couteau	luh koo-to	knife
la couverture	la koo-vair-tewr	blanket
le cow-boy	luh koo-boy	cowboy
la craie	la krai	chalk
la cravate	la kra-vat	tie
le crayon	luh kray-o(n)	pencil
le crayon cire	luh kray-o(n) seer	crayon
les crayons cire (m)	lai kraiy-o(n) seer	crayons
la crème	la krem	cream
la crevette	la kruh-vet	shrimp
le crocodile	luh kro-kodeel	crocodile
le croissant	luh krwa-so(n)	crescent
les cubes (m)	lay kewb	toy blocks
la cuillère	la kwee-yair	spoon
la cuisine	la kwee-zeen	kitchen
la cuisinière	la kwee-zeen-yair	stove

d			
découper	day-koopay	to cut
le dentifrice	luh do(n)tee-freess	toothpaste
les dents (f)	lay do(n)	teeth
le derrière	luh dair-yair	bottom (part of the body)
dessiner	desee-nay	to draw
deux	duh	two
le dindon	luh da(n)-do(n)	turkey
dix	deess	ten
dix-huit	deez-weet	eighteen
dix-neuf	deez-nerf	nineteen
dix-sept	deessett	seventeen
le docteur	luh dokter	doctor
le doigt	luh dwa	finger
dormir	dor-meer	to sleep
le dos	luh dow	back (part of the body)
la douche	la doosh	shower
douze	dooz	twelve

e			
l'eau (f)	lo	water
l'écharpe (f)	lesharp	scarf
l'école (f)	lek-ol	school
écrire	aykreer	to write

l'éléphant (m)	*lelayfo(n)*	elephant
l'entrée (f)	*lo(n)tray*	hall
les épinards (m)	*lay-zepeenar*	spinach
l'éponge (f)	*lepo(n)j*	sponge
l'escalier (m)	*leskal-yay*	stairs
l'escargot (m)	*leskar-go*	snail
l'étau (m)	*letto*	vise
l'étoile (f)	*letwal*	star
être assis	*etr assee*	to be sitting
être debout	*etr duhboo*	to be standing
l'évier (m)	*lev-yay*	sink

f
faire signe	*fair seen-yuh*	to wave
faire du vélo	*fair dew vaylo*	to cycle
la famille	*la fa-mee-yuh*	family
la farine	*la fa-reen*	flour
le fauteuil	*luh fotuh-yuh*	armchair
le fauteuil roulant	*luh fotuh-yuh roolo(n)*	wheelchair
la fenêtre	*la fuh-netr*	window
le fer à repasser	*luh faira-ruhpassay*	iron
la ferme	*la fairm*	farm
la fermeture éclair	*la fairmuh-tewr eklair*	zipper
le fermier	*luh fairm-yay*	farmer
la fête	*la fait*	party
la feuille	*la fer-yuh*	leaf
le feutre	*luh fuh-tr*	felt-tip pen
la ficelle	*la fee-sell*	string
la fille	*la fee-yuh*	girl/daughter
le fils	*luh feess*	son
la fleur	*la fler*	flower
la flûte	*la flewt*	recorder
les formes (f)	*lay form*	shapes
le four à micro-ondes	*luh foor a meekro-o(n)d*	microwave
la fourchette	*la foorshett*	fork
la fourmi	*la foormee*	ant
la fraise	*la frez*	strawberry
la framboise	*la fro(m)-bwuz*	raspberry
le frère	*luh frair*	brother
les frites (f)	*lay freet*	chips
le fromage	*luh frommaj*	cheese
la fusée	*la few-zay*	rocket

g
le gant	*luh gu(n)*	glove
le garçon	*luh gar-so(n)*	boy
le gâteau	*luh ga-to*	cake
le genou	*luh juh-noo*	knee
le gilet	*luh jee-lay*	cardigan
la girafe	*la jee-raf*	giraffe
la glace	*la glass*	ice cream
la gomme	*la gom*	eraser
les graines (f)	*lay grenn*	seeds
la grand-mère	*la gro(n)-mair*	grandmother
le grand-père	*luh gro(n)-pair*	grandfather
la grange	*la gro(n)j*	barn
le grenier	*luh gruhn-yay*	attic
le grille-pain	*luh greeyuh-pa(n)*	toaster
gris	*gree*	gray
la guitare	*la gee-tarr*	guitar

h
le hamburger	*luh a(m)boor-ger*	hamburger
les haricots verts (m)	*lay areeko vair*	green beans
l'hélicoptère (m)	*lellee-koptair*	helicopter
l'hôpital (m)	*lo-peetal*	hospital
le hot-dog	*luh ot-dog*	hotdog
huit	*weet*	eight

i
l'instituteur (m)	*la(n)stee-tewter*	teacher (male)
l'interrupteur (m)	*la(n)terrewp-ter*	switch

j
la jambe	*la jo(m)b*	leg
le jambon	*luh jo(m)bo(n)*	ham
le jardin	*luh jarda(n)*	yard
le jardin public	*luh jarda(n) pewbleek*	park
jaune	*joan*	yellow
le jean	*luh djeen*	jeans
jouer au ballon	*joo-ay o ballo(n)*	to play with a ball
les jouets (m)	*lay joo-ay*	toys
le journal	*luh joor-nal*	newspaper
les jumelles (f)	*lay jew-mell*	binoculars
la jupe	*la jewp*	skirt
le jus de fruits	*luh jew duh frwee*	fruit juice

k
le ketchup	*luh ketchup*	ketchup
le kiwi	*luh kee-wee*	kiwi

l
le lait	*luh lay*	milk
la laitue	*la letew*	lettuce
le lampadaire	*luh lo(m)pa-dair*	street lamp
la lampe	*la lo(m)p*	lamp
le landau	*luh lo(n)do*	baby buggy
la langue	*la long*	tongue
le lapin	*luh la-pa(n)*	rabbit
le lavabo	*luh la-vabbo*	sink
le lave-linge	*luh lav-la(n)j*	washing machine
le lave-vaisselle	*luh lav-vessell*	dishwasher
la lettre	*la letr*	letter
la limace	*la lee-mass*	slug
le lion	*luh lee-o(n)*	lion
le liquide vaisselle	*luh leekeed vessell*	dish soap
lire	*leer*	to read
le lit	*luh lee*	bed
le livre	*luh leevr*	book
les lunettes (f)	*lay lewn-et*	glasses
les lunettes de soleil (f)	*lay lewn-et duh sol-ay*	sunglasses

m
la machine à coudre	*la masheen a kood-ruh*	sewing machine
les magasins (m)	*lay magga-za(n)*	stores
le magazine	*luh maga-zeenn*	magazine
le magnétophone	*luh man-yet-o-fon*	tape recorder
le magnétoscope	*luh man-yet-o-skop*	VCR
le maillot de bain	*luh ma-yo duh ba(n)*	swimsuit
le maillot de corps	*luh ma-yo duh kor*	undershirt
le maillot deux-pièces	*luh ma-yo duh pyes*	bikini
la main	*la ma(n)*	hand
le maïs	*luh ma-eess*	corn
la maison	*la may-zo(n)*	house
manger	*mo(n)jay*	to eat
la mangue	*la mong*	mango
le manteau	*luh mo(n)to*	coat
marcher	*mar-shay*	to walk
la mare	*la mar*	pond
la marionnette	*la ma-ree-onett*	puppet
marron	*ma-ro(n)*	brown
le marteau	*luh mar-to*	hammer
le melon	*luh muhlo(n)*	melon
la mère	*la mair*	mother
le miel	*luh mee-ell*	honey
la mini-chaîne	*la mee-nee-shen*	stereo
le miroir	*luh meer-wahr*	mirror
monter à cheval	*montay a shuhval*	to go horse riding
la montgolfière	*la mo(n)golf-yair*	hot air balloon
la montre	*la mo(n)tr*	watch
la moquette	*la mo-kett*	carpet
la moto	*la moto*	motorcycle
la moutarde	*la moo-tard*	mustard
le mouton	*luh moo-to(n)*	sheep

n

neuf	*nerf*	nine
le nez	*luh nay*	nose
la niche	*la neesh*	doghouse
le nid	*luh nee*	nest
noir	*nwar*	black
la noix de coco	*la nwa duh koko*	coconut
les nombres (m)	*lay no(m)br*	numbers
le nombril	*luh nombreel*	belly button
la nourriture	*la nooree-tewr*	food

o

l'oeil (m)	*ler-yuh*	eye
l'œuf (m)	*lerf*	egg
l'oie (f)	*lwa*	goose
l'oignon (m)	*lonn-yo(n)*	onion
l'oiseau (m)	*lwa-zo*	bird
les oiseaux (m)	*lay-zwazo*	birds
onze	*o(n)z*	eleven
l'orange (f)	*loro(n)j*	orange (fruit)
orange	*oro(n)j*	orange (color)
l'ordinateur (m)	*lordee-na-ter*	computer
l'oreille (f)	*loraye*	ear
l'oreiller (m)	*loray-yay*	pillow
l'os (m)	*loss*	bone
l'ours en peluche (m)	*loorss o(n) plewsh*	teddy bear
les ours en peluche (m)	*layzoorss o(n) plewsh*	teddy bears
l'ovale (m)	*lo-val*	oval

p

la paille	*la pie*	(drinking) straw
le pain	*luh pa(n)*	bread
le pamplemousse	*luh po(m)pl-mooss*	grapefruit
le pantalon	*luh po(n)-ta-lo(n)*	pants
la pantoufle	*la po(n)toofl*	slipper
le papier	*luh pap-yay*	paper
le papier WC	*luh pap-yay vay-say*	toilet paper
le papillon	*luh pa-pee-yo(n)*	butterfly
le papillon	*luh pa-pee-yo(n)*	moth
de nuit	*duh nwee*	
le parapluie	*luh pa-ra-plwee*	umbrella
le parking	*luh par-keeng*	parking lot
la passoire	*la pa-swar*	strainer
la pastèque	*la pastek*	watermelon
la pataugeoire	*la pato-jwar*	wading pool
les pâtes (f)	*lay patt*	pasta
la pêche	*la pesh*	peach (fruit)
le peigne	*luh penn-yuh*	comb
le peignoir	*luh payn-war*	bathrobe
peindre	*pa(n)dr*	to paint
la peinture	*la pa(n)-tewr*	paint
la pelle à ordures	*la pell a ordewr*	dustpan
la pelleteuse	*la pell-terz*	bulldozer
la pellicule photo	*la peleekewl fotto*	film (camera)
la pendule	*la po(n)dewl*	clock
le père	*luh pair*	father
la petite-fille	*la puh-teet-fee-yuh*	granddaughter
le petit-fils	*luh puh-tee-feess*	grandson
les petits pois (m)	*lay puh-tee pwa*	peas
la pharmacie	*la farmassee*	pharmacy
la photo	*la foto*	photograph
le piano	*luh pee-anno*	piano
le pied	*luh pee-ay*	foot
le piment rouge	*luh pee-mo(n) rooj*	chili pepper
le pinceau	*luh pa(n)-so*	paintbrush
le pirate	*luh pee-rat*	pirate
la piscine	*la pee-seen*	swimming pool
la pizza	*la peetza*	pizza
la planche à repasser	*la plo(n)sh a ruh-passay*	ironing board
la planche à roulettes	*la plo(n)sh a roollett*	skateboard
la plante verte	*la plo(n)t vairt*	plant
le plateau	*luh pla-to*	tray

pleurer	*pluh-ray*	to cry
la poêle	*la pwel*	frying pan
la poignée	*la pwan-yay*	door handle
la poire	*la pwar*	pear
le poireau	*luh pwa-ro*	leek
le poisson	*luh pwa-so(n)*	fish
la poitrine fumée	*la pwa-treen few-may*	bacon
le poivre	*luh pwavr*	pepper
le poivron	*luh pwa-vro(n)*	bell pepper
la pomme	*la pom*	apple
la pomme de terre	*la pom duh tair*	potato
les pommes (f)	*lay pom*	apples
le pompier	*luh po(m)p-yay*	fireman
le pont	*luh po(n)*	bridge
le pop-corn	*luh pop-korn*	popcorn
la porte	*la port*	door
le portemanteau	*luh port-mo(n)to*	peg (for clothes)
le porte-monnaie	*luh port monnay*	coin purse
la poste	*la post*	post office
le pot	*luh po*	can/potty chair
le pot de fleurs	*luh po duh fler*	flowerpot
la poubelle	*la poobell*	trash can
le pouce	*luh pooss*	thumb
la poule	*la pool*	hen
le poulet	*luh poollay*	chicken
la poupée	*la poo-pay*	doll
pousser	*poossay*	to push
la poussette	*la poossett*	stroller
le poussin	*luh poossa(n)*	chick
la prune	*la prewn*	plum
le pull-over	*luh pewlo-vair*	sweater
le puzzle	*luh puhzl*	jigsaw puzzle
le pyjama	*luh pee-jama*	pajamas

q

quatorze	*ka-torz*	fourteen
quatre	*katr*	four
quinze	*ka(n)z*	fifteen

r

la radio	*la rad-yo*	radio
le raisin	*luh ray-za(n)*	grapes
les raisins secs (m)	*lai ray-za(n) sek*	raisins
la rampe	*la ro(m)p*	banister
la raquette de tennis	*la rakett duh teneess*	tennis racket
le râteau	*luh ra-to*	rake
le rectangle	*luh rek-to(n)gl*	rectangle
le réfrigérateur	*luh refree-jaira-ter*	refrigerator
la règle	*la regl*	ruler
le réveil	*luh rev-ay*	alarm clock
le rideau	*luh ree-do*	curtain
rire	*reer*	to laugh
le riz	*luh ree*	rice
la robe	*la rob*	dress
le robinet	*luh robbee-nay*	faucet
le robot	*luh robbo*	robot
rose	*roz*	pink
la roue	*la roo*	wheel
rouge	*rooj*	red
le ruban	*luh rewbo(n)*	ribbon
le ruban adhésif	*luh rewbo(n) a-dezeef*	tape
la rue	*la rew*	street

s

le sac à dos	*luh sakka-do*	backpack
le sachet de thé	*luh sa-shay duh tay*	tea bag
la salle de bains	*la sal duh ba(n)*	bathroom
la salle de classe	*la sal de klas*	classroom
la salle de séjour	*la sal duh sejoor*	living room

la salopette	*la salopette*	overalls
la sandale	*la so(n)dal*	sandal
le sandwich	*luh so(n)d-weech*	sandwich
la saucisse	*la so-seess*	sausage
le saucisson	*luh so-see-so(n)*	salami
sauter	*so-tay*	to jump
le savon	*luh sa-vo(n)*	soap
la scie	*la see*	saw
se laver	*suh la-vai*	to wash (yourself)
le seau	*luh so*	bucket
seize	*sez*	sixteen
le sel	*luh sell*	salt
s'embrasser	*sombrassay*	to kiss (each other)
sept	*sett*	seven
le serpent	*luh sair-po(n)*	snake
le serveur	*luh sairv-er*	waiter
la serviette	*la sairv-yet*	towel
le shampooing	*luh shompweng*	shampoo
la sirène	*la see-ren*	mermaid
six	*seess*	six
le slip	*luh sleep*	underpants
le slip de bain	*luh sleep duh ba(n)*	swimming trunks
la soeur	*la ser*	sister
la soucoupe	*la soo-koop*	saucer
la soupe	*la soop*	soup
sourire	*sooreer*	to smile
la souris	*lay soo-ree*	computer mouse/mouse
les souris	*lay soo-ree*	mice
le sous-marin	*luh soo-ma-ra(n)*	submarine
la station-service	*la sta-see-o(n) ser-vees*	gas station
le store	*luh stor*	blind
le stylo à encre	*luh stee-lo a o(n)kr*	ink pen
les stylos (m)	*lay stee-lo*	pens
le sucre	*luh sewkr*	sugar
le supermarché	*luh sew-pair-mar-shay*	supermarket
le survêtement	*luh sewr-vetmo(n)*	sweat suit
le sweat-shirt	*luh sweat-shert*	sweatshirt

t

la table	*la tabl*	table
la table de nuit	*la tabl duh nwee*	night stand
le tableau	*luh taa-blo*	board
le tablier	*luh ta-blee-ay*	apron
le tabouret	*luh ta-boo-ray*	stool
le taille-crayon	*luh tie-yuh kray-o(n)*	pencil sharpener
le tambour	*luh to(m)-boor*	drum
le tambourin	*luh to(m)-boo-ra(n)*	tambourine
le tapis	*luh ta-pee*	rug
la tasse	*la tass*	cup
les tasses (f)	*lay tass*	cups

le taureau	*luh taw-raw*	bull
le taxi	*luh tax-ee*	taxi
le tee-shirt	*luh tee-shert*	T-shirt
le téléphérique	*luh tellay-fair-eek*	ski lift
le téléphone	*luh tellay-fon*	telephone
la télévision	*luh tellay-veez-yo(n)*	television
la tente	*la tont*	tent
la tête	*la tet*	head
tirer	*teer-ay*	to pull
le toboggan	*luh to-bo-go(n)*	slide
les toilettes (f)	*lay twa-lett*	toilet
le toit	*luh twa*	roof
la tomate	*la to-mat*	tomato
les tomates (f)	*lay to-mat*	tomatoes
la tondeuse	*la to(n)-derz*	lawnmower
la torche	*la torsh*	flashlight
le tournevis	*luh toor-nuh-veess*	screwdriver
le tourniquet	*luh toor-neekay*	merry-go-round
le tracteur	*luh trak-ter*	tractor
le train	*luh tra(n)*	train
les tranports (m)	*lay tro(n)-spor*	transportation
treize	*trez*	thirteen
le triangle	*luh tree-o(n)gl*	triangle
trois	*trwa*	three
la trompette	*la tro(m)-pet*	trumpet
la trottinette	*la tro-tee-net*	scooter
le tuyau d'arrosage	*luh twee-yo da-ro-zaj*	hose

u

un	*a(n)*	one

v

la vache	*la vash*	cow
le vaisseau spatial	*luh vesso spa-see-al*	spaceship
la valise	*la va-leez*	suitcase
le vase	*luh vaz*	vase
le veau	*luh vo*	calf
le vélo	*luh velo*	bike
le ventre	*luh vo(n)tr*	belly
le ver de terre	*luh vair duh tair*	worm
les vers de terre (m)	*lay vair duh tair*	worms
vert	*vair*	green
les vêtements (m)	*lay vet-mo(n)*	clothes
la ville	*la veel*	town
vingt	*va(n)*	twenty
violet	*vee-olay*	purple
la voiture	*la vwa-tewr*	car
la voiture de course	*la vwa-tewr duh koorss*	race car
la voiture de police	*la vwa-tewr duh po-leess*	police car
la voiture de sport	*la vwa-tewr duh spor*	sports car
les voitures	*lay vwa-tewr*	cars

y

le yaourt	*luh ya-oort*	yogurt

Additional models: Les Pickstock, Barry Jones, Stef Lumley and Karen Krige. With thanks to Vicki Groombridge, Nicole Irving and the Model Shop, 151 City Road, London.